C.C. Warrens

Every dream starts as a flicker of hope

for something more.

i

To my wonderful readers. Your love of these characters, as well as your encouragement through emails, messages, and reviews mean more to me than you may ever know.

~C.C. Warrens~

Winter Memorial is a short story that takes place between "Criss Cross" and "Cross Fire." I originally wrote it as a Christmas gift to my newsletter subscribers, but since not everyone can (or wants to) subscribe to a newsletter, I wanted to make it available for all of my readers.

I hope you enjoy this extra glimpse into Holly's world.

C.C. Warrens

Published Works

Criss Cross

Winter Memorial (bonus short story)

Cross Fire

Crossed Off

Injustice for All

Holly Jolly Christmas

C.C. Warrens

© 2018 C.C. Warrens

This novel is a work of fiction. Situations, scenarios, and characters in this book are a reflection of creative imagination and not representative of any specific person, group, situation, or event.

Winter Memorial

By C.C. Warrens

One

LIFE IS A TEMPORARY GIFT—a fragile, fleeting moment in time. And when that moment is over, and that person's soul moves on, nothing of them remains but an empty shell and a memory.

That was Jace's fear as she held her brother's hand. Machines kept his heart beating and his lungs breathing, but she couldn't help but wonder if his moment was over.

"Do you think he's gone?" she asked, her voice tight with unshed tears. She looked over at her best friend, who sat beside her next to the hospital bed.

Holly's eyes shimmered with sympathy, but she had no answer to give. She simply wrapped her fingers around Jace's free hand and squeezed.

Jace's brother, Scott, had been attacked two years ago, the brutality of it leaving him in a coma. The doctors said there was little chance of recovery, but God wasn't confined by the same limitations as doctors.

Jace returned Holly's gentle squeeze before gazing at her brother. His black hair and slightly curved eyes—attributes passed on by their mother's Asian heritage—were so like her own.

"I miss you, baby brother," she whispered, tears pooling in her blue eyes.

If she could have one wish, it would be to have him back. He had never treated her differently after the car accident that stole her ability to walk. Her father didn't know how to interact with her now, and there was always disappointment in her mother's eyes, as if Jace had chosen to disrupt her mother's plans for her future.

Scott had never loved her differently. He had simply hugged her and told her they would get through this. He was the one who encouraged her to join the adaptive sports program—the organization that allowed her to play sled hockey and wheelchair basketball.

A quiet tap on the door drew their attention. Sam stood in the doorway, his police uniform traded in for a pair of jeans and a sweater. He was a solid five-foot-eight with Latino features that made a lot of women take a second glance.

Holly was immune to his good looks, as she was with most men, but Jace had fallen head over wheels the first time he offered to walk her back to her apartment.

Sam had been one of the three officers who volunteered to watch over Holly that past fall. He acknowledged her with a slight nod, and she gave him a little finger wave.

Jace wiped the tears from her face, and some of her grief slid away at the sight of her boyfriend. "Hey. I was gonna come over after our visit."

Sam leaned against the door frame. "I had time to stop by before the banquet. How's he doing?"

Jace's expression sobered, and Holly chimed in. "He looks healthier today. His cheeks are pink."

Jace searched her brother's face for the hopeful changes Holly saw. Maybe there was a bit of pink to his cheeks, but she couldn't be sure.

"I'm glad to hear it," Sam said.

"Hey, you're wearing the sweater I got you," Jace realized. A grin spread slowly across her face, bringing back the fiery sparkle that usually filled her eyes. "I knew you'd look sexy in red."

Holly let out a soft snort of amusement, and Sam arched an eyebrow at her. She donned an innocent expression, as if to say, "What? It wasn't me."

Jace rolled her eyes. "Ignore her. She doesn't think any guy is attractive. The last super cute guy who asked her out, and even bought her a muffin, she turned down flat."

Holly shrugged. "He . . . wasn't my type."

"If you don't find Sam, Jordan, or Mr. Southern attractive, there's something wrong with you."

One eyebrow crept slowly up Sam's forehead. "You think Marx is attractive?"

Jace flashed him a grin. "In a southern cornbread kind of way."

"That's disturbing," Sam said, but he didn't sound genuinely bothered.

Marx was a friend as well as a detective at his precinct, and he was a few years shy of fifty. He was also only romantically interested in one woman—his ex-wife—and he showed no signs of moving on.

"Are the two of you still planning on coming to the memorial tonight?" Sam asked.

"Oh my gosh, is it time to get ready already?" Jace panicked.

Sam glanced at his watch. "It's still three hours away. Relax."

Jace frowned at him. "You say that like it's a lot of time. I'll spend half that time just trying to convince Holly to wear a dress, and then we'll have to get it *on* her, which is like, an exercise in the impossible. And then there's the stilettos and makeup."

Holly might be naturally beautiful, but she dressed to blend in with the wallpaper. She lived her life in jeans and layered T-shirts, and she looked at a mascara brush like it was a torture device.

Granted, Jace *had* accidentally poked her in the eye with it the one time she used it, so . . . maybe that was a legitimate concern.

"I can dress myself," Holly objected, getting to her feet.

Jace gave her an incredulous look. "If you show up in blue jeans and sneakers, I will literally scream." She didn't miss the flicker of hesitation on Holly's face, and she pounced on it. "Ha! I knew it. That's what you were planning to wear."

Holly folded her arms and said indignantly, "I have shoes that aren't sneakers."

"What about a dress?"

"I'm not wearing a dress."

Jace shot Sam a *help me* look, and he shook his head. "I don't get involved in women's wardrobe disputes."

Jace sighed. "At least wear the stilettos I got you. A few more inches of height wouldn't kill you."

The shoes might, Holly thought, visions of falling down steps and tripping over thin air playing through her mind. No, she definitely wasn't wearing stilettos.

Two

HOLLY'S FOOT SLIPPED on a patch of ice on the walkway, and she nearly hit the ground. Marx caught her and set her back on her feet.

"Thanks," she said, heart thumping wildly. She stepped away from him, craving her space, and shot a scalding look at the patch of ice that should've instantly liquefied it.

"Probably not the best winter shoes," Marx pointed out, nodding down at the pair of sparkly red flats on her feet.

Holly looked down at her feet and frowned. "But everyone said I was supposed to dress nice."

Marx smiled. Holly's idea of nice differed from most people's. For a formal banquet, most women would wear an evening dress and a pair of heels or dress boots. Holly chose red flats, black skinny jeans, and a red sweater that was at least a size too big.

"You look fine," Marx said, resisting the urge to point out that by dressing to go unnoticed, her casual attire was going to make her the most noticeable person at the banquet.

Tonight was a formal occasion to honor the officers New York City had lost in 2016—far too many—and all the officers in attendance would be wearing their dress blues, including Marx.

As they approached the front doors of the building, Holly quickened her pace and snatched the handle of the door before anyone else could. She flung the door wide and exclaimed triumphantly, "Ha!"

She had been trying to get to the door first for months, but Marx always managed to get there first.

"Really? That's how it's gonna be this evenin'?" he asked. At her grin, he added, "Don't you dare pull out my chair in front of the other officers."

She had pulled his chair out for him once before just to get back at him for always opening her door.

Mischief glinted in her eyes. "No promises."

Marx shook his head in amusement and gripped the door well above her head. He let Jace and Sam enter first, then gestured Holly inside. "Well go on."

She rolled her eyes and stepped into the warm building. Marx did a quick visual sweep of the parking lot, searching for Holly's unwanted shadow. He had yet to make an appearance since he called on her birthday, but it was only a matter of time.

Marx doubted he would have the guts to come for her at a police banquet; he wouldn't be able to drag her more than an inch without someone body-checking him. He would be in a jail cell before the night was over.

They walked into the crowded banquet hall, and an employee came to collect their coats. Holly regarded the man with suspicion. She didn't trust strangers with her belongings.

Or her food.

Marx barely restrained a laugh when she pulled a sandwich bag of marshmallows from her coat pocket before handing the coat over. "You brought marshmallows to a banquet?"

"For dessert," she said, her tone suggesting the reason was obvious.

"It's a *banquet*, Holly. I'm sure they'll have dessert."

Her eyes lit up with interest, and she looked around the room for the dessert table. Marx shook his head. It was a wonder, given the amount of junk food she ate, that she was as tiny as she was.

He kept an eye on her as he shook hands with fellow officers and greeted their wives. He was concerned about how Holly might cope in a room full of people, most of them cops, and many of them men.

But she had insisted on apologizing to Jacob's parents. Marx supposed that was his fault. After Jacob was killed in the line of duty outside Holly's apartment, he had said a lot of things in anger that he shouldn't have, including making her feel guilty that Jacob's parents had lost their only child.

Holly was a compassionate person, and of everything he said that day, that was the one detail she held onto. She had lost her parents, and Jacob's parents had lost their child. Nothing he said would convince her to stay home.

He felt her step a hair closer to him, practically vibrating with anxiety, and he searched the room for the source.

A group of three male officers were regarding her with interest. Marx wasn't surprised—she was a pretty, single girl—but he knew their attention wasn't welcome. When one of the officers broke away from the group to approach her, Marx shook his head.

The young officer paused mid-step, confusion flashing across his face. He looked between Marx and Holly a few times, drew his own conclusions, and backed off.

Wise decision, Marx thought.

He didn't want Holly getting spooked and bolting out the front door. The streets weren't the safest place for her right now, especially after dark.

An older man, in his sixties with hair that was fading to snow, made his way through the crowd toward them. McNera was not only the precinct captain, but Marx's oldest friend. They had been partners when both of them were nothing more than beat cops.

"Good evenin', sir," Marx said.

McNera clapped him on the shoulder. "Glad you could make it." He shook Sam's hand, and then considered the woman by his side. "And who is this beautiful young lady?" he asked, offering his hand to her.

"This is Jace," Sam said. "My girlfriend."

McNera enclosed Jace's hand with both of his. "If I weren't happily married, my dear, I would ask you out for coffee."

Jace beamed at the compliment.

"Always the charmer," an older woman said as she came up behind McNera. Her voice was filled with lighthearted amusement, as if she knew the compliment went no deeper than polite flattery. "He said something similar to me once. In front of my father."

"And then he chased me off the property," McNera mused. He wrapped an arm around the woman and kissed her cheek, love overflowing with every gesture. "You should've seen his reaction when I asked for her hand. I barely escaped with my life. Everyone, this stunning beauty is my wife, Margaret."

Margaret smiled, and her brown eyes twinkled. "Pleasure to meet you all. If you'll excuse us. We have a few more people to greet." She swept her husband away toward the entry doors.

Marx looked down at Holly. "You ready to find Jacob's family?"

She nodded, but he could see the apprehension in her eyes. She was worried about how they would react to her, but Marx knew Pat and Sally well. Even if they held Holly responsible for their son's death, which he doubted, they would never let her know it.

Three

HIS PALMS BROKE OUT WITH SWEAT when he saw her enter the banquet hall. She looked no different than he remembered—black hair with frosted blue tips—and it brought the past rushing up beneath his feet.

He could still smell the coppery scent of blood in the air and hear the laughter all around him. None of them had set out that night with violence in mind, but sometimes the night took on a life of its own. Too much booze mixed with too much stupidity, and someone always paid the price.

He closed his eyes, trying to blot out the memories, but it only sharpened them.

The dark street unfolded behind his eyelids, the lamps buzzing and flickering overhead. There was a chill to the air, and he watched his breath disappear in clouds of steam. He should've been watching where he was walking, because he tripped over a bottle one of the others tossed onto the road and sprawled on the pavement.

He heard their laughter over the dull buzzing between his ears.

"What's the matter, Gav? Too much to drink?" one of his friends teased.

Vic crouched beside him, his stringy hair covering half of his face. "I've seen eighth grade girls drink more than you and stay on their feet." He smacked Gavin's cheek hard. "Don't be such a wuss."

Gavin started to push himself up, but Vic kicked one of his arms out from under him and he fell back to the pavement.

"Woops!" Vic said, cackling. "You're so fat you can't even get off the ground. Come on, Pillsbury, give it another try. Maybe this time . . ."

Vic's voice trailed off, and Gavin was afraid to know what that meant, but then he followed his attention to a girl walking down the sidewalk. He flinched when Vic stepped over him and started toward her.

He had a sick feeling in the pit of his stomach that Vic was going to hurt her, but at the same time, he was relieved to be momentarily forgotten. The girl became the target of Vic's drunken hunt for fun, until *he* came rushing in to help her.

The events of the night blurred into a soundtrack of screams and shouts, punctuated by flashes of violence. They had nearly killed the guy who stepped in to help the girl. He may as well be dead. He was a vegetable lying in a hospital bed, with no hope of ever recovering.

Gavin opened his eyes and stared across the banquet hall at the woman in the wheelchair, the woman who had cried out on the news for witnesses to come forward about her brother's attack.

No one had come forward, not even the girl. He remembered the sense of relief that had washed through him as months passed without consequences: no form of retaliation, no cops coming to knock down the door and drag them off to prison. They were free.

But Gavin felt anything but free.

Guilt was more of a prison than any jail cell would ever be. There was no escaping these bars, no hope of early release. He would be trapped for the rest of his life.

One of the other employees carried over the pile of jackets he had collected from the group the woman was with, and Gavin stared at the blue coat she'd been wearing.

Maybe there was something he could do to ease the weight of his guilt. Some small thing . . .

Four

PAT LOOKED LIKE THE fifty-year-old version of his son Jacob—a boyish face despite his graying hair, and an athletic build that spoke of marathon training—and Sally was very much the opposite, with a weary face and plump figure.

"Pat, Sally," Marx said as he and Holly emerged from the throng of people in the center of the room.

Sally stepped forward to hug him. "It's so good to see you. We've missed seeing you since the funeral."

Marx hugged her back. "I'm sorry I've been so busy."

"Oh, that's understandable," she said, releasing him. "But we would love to have you over for dinner sometime. You and Sam. You both meant so much to Jake."

Pat slapped him on the shoulder affectionately. "It's good to see you, Richard. I don't know that we ever thanked you for what you did for our son. You taught him a lot, took him under your wing. You were his hero on the police force."

Jacob had been the closest thing to a son Marx would ever have, and he had to clear the emotion from his throat before speaking. "This is Holly, the young lady Jacob helped us protect this past fall."

Sally and Pat turned their attention to the young woman standing unobtrusively off to the side. Sally pressed fingers to her lips as tears misted her eyes. "Oh, Holly, thank you for coming. We were so hoping to meet you."

Holly blinked, seeming unsure how to react to her kindness, and looked up at Marx for some kind of cue. He gestured for her to tell them what was on her mind.

She fidgeted, clearly uncomfortable being the center of attention. "I just wanted to say, um . . . that I'm sorry . . . f-for what happened. I never wanted . . . anyone to get hurt, and I'm so sorry."

She wrapped her arms around herself, and Marx had a feeling she was remembering Jacob's body lying on her kitchen floor. It was an image he couldn't erase from his mind, either.

"Oh, honey," Sally said, pulling Holly into a tight hug before Marx could tell her that was a bad idea. Holly stiffened, but Sally didn't seem to notice. "We don't blame you for what happened that night, and neither would Jake." She pulled back to take Holly in. "He wouldn't regret protecting you. It was who he was."

"He knew what he was getting himself into," Pat added.

"Well, mostly," another man said, inviting himself into the conversation. He had the same jawline and nose as Jacob, but the red-rimmed eyes he fixed on Holly had come from a different set of genes.

Sally shot him a reproachful look. "Keith, now isn't the time."

Keith slid a hand into the pocket of his slacks. "Face it, Aunt Sally. Jake might have known what he was getting himself into, but he should've known better than to fall for the woman he was supposed to be protecting."

Holly's mouth opened, but she couldn't find the words to say. She looked up at Marx in confusion. He had known Jacob was developing feelings for Holly, and he had pulled him aside after one of his shifts to set him straight.

"Oh," Keith said with amusement, swishing the wine around in his glass. "Either she's an actress worthy of an Academy award, or she didn't know little Jake had a thing for her."

"Keith," Pat snapped. "I think you've had enough to drink."

"It's odd though. As far back as I can remember, Jake always fell for the tall brunettes with more selfies than brain cells." Keith gestured toward Holly with his glass of wine. "I'm curious what happened here. Is nobody else curious?"

Marx had never met Jacob's cousin, but he'd heard about him. The two had been close as boys, but their paths had diverged when they reached their twenties. Marx glanced at Sally, who had a hand pressed to her forehead in stress.

"Why don't you find another corner to drink in," Marx suggested to Keith, keeping his tone as polite as possible under the circumstances.

Keith smiled. "You know, I bet it's her looks. Aunt Sally, doesn't she remind you of one of those porcelain dolls you collect? Pale and pretty with big eyes and long hair. It's like she stepped right off the shelf."

Pat took the glass of wine from him. "Why don't you get some fresh air."

"Why? I'm just getting to know the woman who got my best friend and cousin killed all in the same day."

Holly flinched, and Marx's irritation spiked. Keith might be grieving for his cousin, but that didn't give him the right to hurt Holly. "Come on, sweetheart," Marx said, directing her back the way they had come.

"Oh yes, run away," Keith called after them. "Wouldn't want to answer questions!"

Marx gritted his teeth. He wanted to turn around and slap the man sober, but he wouldn't lose his temper in front of Holly.

Pat said something to Keith in low tones, which only seem to fuel Keith's antics. "I have a right to ask questions. She spent more time with Jake the last two months of his life than his own family. I wanna know what happened all the days he was there. Should I be expecting another cousin in the next six months? Look at that sweater! She's clearly dressing for two."

Holly stumbled as she looked back at him, her eyes wide.

"Just ignore him. He's drunk," Marx suggested. He escorted her back to Sam and Jace, and said, "I'll be back in a minute. I'm gonna go help Keith find the exit."

Holly looked down at her sweater, then shot a quizzical glance at Sam and Jace. "Do I look pregnant?"

Five

THE THREE OF THEM WATCHED as Marx *escorted* Keith out of the main room. Holly slid a glance at Sam.

"Is he allowed to just drag people away like that?"

Sam tilted his head and gave a vague grunt. "Considering the guy was disrupting the memorial banquet for fallen officers, I don't think anyone's gonna intervene on his behalf."

Holly shaped a silent "oh" with her lips, and glanced back in the direction of Jacob's parents. This night would be difficult enough for them without their nephew's drunken displays.

Jace let out a frustrated sound, drawing Sam and Holly's attention. She was searching through her purse, shoving stuff back and forth.

"Jace, what are you looking for?" Sam asked. She was going to rip out the lining of her purse if she didn't find it soon.

"My phone. I swear I had it in my purse, but . . ." She let out another growling sound and shook her massive bag. "It has to be in here."

"Or it could be in your coat," he said.

She looked up. "My coat. Why didn't I think of that?"

"Because frustration turns your brain to mush?" Holly offered. Jace stuck her tongue out at her, and Holly grinned. "I'll go check your coat."

Sam drew in a breath to object—he was supposed to keep an eye on her in Marx's absence—but then decided to let it go. She was only going across the room.

Holly slipped and ducked her way through the crowded room, letting out a breath of relief when she stepped into the alcove where the employee had taken their coats. She had room to breathe and move without running into someone.

She no sooner thought that when someone in white bumped into her with enough force to knock her off her feet. She landed on the floor with a startled squeak and watched the heavy-set man in a white waiter's jacket dash through the door into the kitchen.

She blew a tuft of hair out of her face and glared after him. As she started to get to her feet, a hand wrapped around her arm. She pulled away instinctively, and nearly took the other person back to the floor with her.

"Easy," the woman said, digging her heels in. "I'm just trying to give you a hand up." She pulled Holly to her feet, and waited for her to find her balance before letting go.

"Sorry," Holly said, her heart pounding. She was surprised to see that the woman—scarcely taller than her—was wearing the same uniform as the other officers. She had nearly tackled a police officer to the floor. Could they arrest her for that?

"Guy knocked you off your feet pretty hard. You good?"

Holly nodded. "I'm okay. Thanks."

She didn't notice the wall of male officers waiting to pounce until the woman turned to them and said, "She's fine. You guys don't have to kill anyone. Go back to your conversation about football."

The men chuckled softly before dispersing.

"Men," the woman grunted. She looked Holly over. "Gotta learn to plant your feet when you're a woman our size. Otherwise people just bowl you over."

Holly looked down at her feet, which looked pretty planted to her. "Okay," she said, still confused. "Thanks . . ."

"Name's Nance. Watch out for through traffic next time, okay?" She offered Holly a smile that crinkled the corners of her eyes, then rejoined her comrades.

Holly puffed out a breath and turned to look for Jace's coat. It was the brightest spec of color in a sea of grays and blacks. She dug through the pockets until she found the phone.

A slip of paper fluttered to the floor when she pulled the phone out. As she bent to pick it up, she noticed there was something written on it: *sry 4 ur bro.*

She assumed it was supposed to read: *sorry for your brother.* Would it really kill people to take an extra half a second to write the other letters? Good grief.

As she read the message again, her thoughts turned to Scott. What were the chances that the wording of this note was a coincidence? Or that it had been placed in the wrong person's coat pocket?

Something didn't feel right.

She turned to look in the direction the waiter had disappeared. He had been in an awfully big hurry. She shoved the note into the pocket of her jeans and walked through the door into the kitchen.

Six

SAM GLANCED AT HIS WATCH. "It doesn't take that much time to get over there and back. What's taking her so long?"

Jace shrugged. "Maybe she met a cute guy along the way. What's with the worry?"

"I'm not worried," he lied. A small commotion broke out on the other side of the room, and he frowned. "I'll be right back."

"Sure, everybody just leave me," Jace muttered. "I don't have any abandonment issues from like . . . my whole family or anything."

Sam kissed her forehead and said, "I'm not abandoning you. For long. I'll be back in a second."

She melted under his warm kiss and smiled. "Go do your cop thing. I'll be here when you get back."

He left to find out what had caused the stir, but by the time he reached the other side, everything was calm. He searched the alcove where Holly was supposed to be, but it was empty.

He caught one of the other officers. "What happened?"

The cop swallowed the bite of pie he had just taken. "Some waiter knocked a girl over. Guess he was in a big hurry 'cause he didn't say sorry or nothin'. Just booked it into the kitchen."

"What girl?"

"Red hair. Big sweater."

"Where'd she go?"

"Kitchen."

Sam frowned. "With the guy who knocked her over?"

"No, she went *after* the guy who knocked her over. Maybe she wants an apology." The officer shrugged. "I don't try to figure women out."

"Thanks." Sam pulled out his cell and dialed Holly's number as he walked into the kitchen. His eyes skimmed over the employees, looking for red hair, but she wasn't there.

His eyes locked on the side door that lead outside. "She wouldn't." He walked to the door and pushed it open. There in the snow were tiny, Holly-sized footprints leading away from the building. "She did."

Her number rolled over to voicemail.

He slid his phone back into his pocket and stepped out into the cold night. The door squeaked shut behind him. One small security light highlighted Holly's tracks in the snow, as well as a much larger, deeper set belonging to a man.

He didn't understand what would compel a woman to follow a man she didn't know outside after dark. Unless she *did* know him. But even then, this was Holly—the woman who was too afraid of men to let them in her apartment.

What are you doing, Holly, he thought with frustration. He rested his hand on his gun as he followed the tracks.

Seven

A WOMAN'S SCREAM shattered the night, and Sam's grip on his gun tightened as he whirled toward the sound. His eyes flicked over the snow-covered street and sidewalks, but he saw no sign of Holly.

She had been drugged and attacked last fall when he was supposed to be protecting her, and he wouldn't let someone hurt her again. Not on his watch.

His pulse jumped when he heard another scream, and he started toward the street. A couple stumbled around the corner of an apartment building, and the woman let out another scream when the man with her swept her off her feet, but this scream ended in laughter.

Sam released a breath of relief, then returned to the tracks in the snow. The footprints lead away from the banquet hall toward the neighboring building.

He heard the beginning of a prayer whispering on the breeze, but he couldn't tell which direction it was coming from.

"God, please . . ." the voice pleaded. The closer he came to the building, the clearer the prayer became. "If I come forward now, I'll go to prison. I can't go to prison. Please, God, tell me what to do."

Sam rounded the building to find a petite woman peering around a storage unit, her arms wrapped around herself as she shivered. Her feet disappeared into snow that brushed the middle of her calves, and she wasn't wearing a coat.

"Holly."

She jumped and looked back at him with wide, startled eyes, then slowly relaxed. "Don't do that."

"You're lucky it's just me and not one of the gang members or sexual predators who frequent this neighborhood." That had been his fear when he heard a woman screaming. "What are you doing out here?"

She pulled a folded piece of paper from her pocket and handed it to him. "I found this in Jace's coat pocket. I think the guy who put it there knows something about her brother. He freaked out when I came into the coat alcove and ran outside."

Sam lifted his eyes from the note. "You think this man, who, by the way, can't even spell the word sorry, might have beaten Jace's brother into a coma two years ago, so you followed him out here by yourself?" He stared at her in disbelief. "You realize he could be violent and disturbed. And judging by these footprints, he's twice your size. What exactly was your plan?"

Holly hesitated. "To . . . talk to him?"

Sam closed his eyes and exhaled a calming breath. He did not understand this woman. "Even if this note happens to be more than a coincidence, which is unlikely, you're not a detective, Holly."

"Neither are you."

"Yes, but I know how to handle myself if a confrontation goes south. You don't. And you're gonna freeze to death out here in what you're wearing."

Holly bounced on her toes to keep warm—at least she thought she was bouncing on her toes. She couldn't really feel them anymore. "If you don't talk to him, I will. Jace deserves to know what happened to her brother."

"I'll talk to him if you go back inside."

She shook her head. "Talk first, then I go inside."

"You're completely irrational."

When she just shrugged, he sighed and stepped around the storage shed to speak to the man, only to find him running, or rather, staggering through the snow as fast as he could.

Was this guy seriously trying to run from the police through the snow at that speed? Sam let out another frustrated breath and set off after him at a relaxed jog.

He caught the guy by the shirt and hauled him to a stop, which wasn't easy given his size. They slid in the snow, and Sam ducked when the big man's arm nearly took his head off. He gave him a hard shove, and the man landed on his back in the snow.

This was exactly why Sam didn't want Holly involved. If the man had swung out at her like that and connected, she would be the one lying in the snow.

As the man lay there, gasping for breath, Sam got a closer look at his face. He couldn't be more than eighteen. He held up the note and said, "We need to talk." He glanced at the nametag pinned to his shirt. "Gavin. And don't bother trying to run again; I'll catch you in two steps."

Eight

GAVIN DROPPED INTO A CHAIR in one of the side rooms and slumped down. He cast a sideways glance at Sam's uniform as he pulled up a chair beside him. "You're a cop."

"You're working a cop's banquet," Sam said. "Were you expecting a priest?"

"I might prefer a priest. They don't usually bring handcuffs."

Sam almost smiled.

Gavin's gaze moved to Holly, who stood in the doorway, and his attention lingered a second too long, the way a teenage boy's attention usually did when a pretty girl walked into a room, and Sam snapped his fingers beside his ear.

Gavin flinched.

"Focus on me, Gavin."

Gavin flushed with embarrassment, and muttered in Holly's direction, "I'm sorry for knocking you down earlier."

"You could've hurt her," Sam pointed out, and Gavin's cheeks brightened even more.

"I didn't mean to."

"Did you mean to take a swing at me outside?"

"You grabbed me, and I just reacted," Gavin explained. "I didn't wanna hurt anyone."

His answers sounded genuine, and Sam had a feeling the kid wouldn't be able to keep a straight face if he lied. "Let's talk about the note."

"I should've never wrote that note," Gavin said, swiping at his runny nose with a sleeve. "But I just wanted her to know I'm sorry."

"Sorry for what?"

"For what happened. For that night. We didn't plan it, I swear. We were just drinking, and things . . . they kinda got outta hand, you know?"

"If by out of hand you mean a man was nearly beaten to death and left in a coma, then yes, I know," Sam said evenly, and Gavin flinched.

"That wasn't supposed to happen. We were just having some fun. But this guy, Vic . . . me and my friends met him at a party, and he seemed okay at first, but later . . ." he shifted in his chair. "There was this girl walking home. She was, uh, slow, I guess. Some kinda mental thing. And Vic, he got the guys riled up, and they were pushing her around and calling her names. Making fun of her. She was crying."

Sam exhaled a slow breath as he imagined a girl with a developmental delay being bullied by a group of guys. She would've been helpless and terrified. "How far did it go?"

Gavin looked at Holly, then slumped further down in his chair. "Does she have to be here?"

"Yes," Sam said. He wasn't making the mistake of letting her out of his sight again. "If you did something wrong, you own up to it, no matter who's listening."

Gavin visibly swallowed. "I didn't hurt the girl. I swear. I didn't even call her names or anything. I would never hurt a girl. But I didn't . . ."

"You didn't help her," Sam said, and Gavin shook his head.

Tears glittered in his eyes. "I know I should've done something, but I was scared. I was only sixteen, the youngest of the group, the fat kid. I was just lucky to be there."

He looked at Holly, as if he needed her, more than Sam, to understand why he hadn't helped the girl. Sam wondered vaguely if he viewed women as more of an authority, or if he just didn't want the pretty girl in the room to think he was a coward.

Holly's expression was conflicted, but she didn't say anything.

"Then that Asian guy came along to help her. And they did to him what I was afraid they would do to me if I tried to stop them." A tear rolled down Gavin's cheek, and he brushed it away with his sleeve. "Vic just kept kicking him. He wasn't even moving anymore, but he wouldn't stop."

Sam saw Holly blink back tears, and he had to suppress his own emotional reaction. This was his girlfriend's brother they were talking about, and he was angry on her behalf. "Did you call the police?"

Gavin shook his head.

"I was so scared I just ran home and hid in my room. My Grams would be so disappointed if she knew."

A disappointed Grandmother would be the least of his problems, but Sam didn't mention that at the moment. "Tell me about the other guys."

"Gone," Gavin said with a shrug. "Joey got pinched for robbing some old couple on his street. He's in prison. Eddy . . . he OD'd on heroin a week after everything happened. I don't know what happened to Vic, and I don't care. As long as he's not here."

Sam absorbed the information and tried to think of a way to break the news to Jace. There was nothing he could say to keep her from tears, but maybe she would take comfort in the fact that her brother was a hero.

"I beg God for forgiveness every day," Gavin said, tears dripping from his chin onto his uniform.

"God might forgive you, but as long as you're on this earth, there are still consequences," Sam replied. He stood and pulled out his handcuffs.

Nine

JACE STRAIGHTENED WHEN SHE SAW Sam approaching. "You said you would be back in a second. That was like the longest second in the history of time. I was seriously about to post some missing person flyers."

Sam didn't smile or even lift an eyebrow at her comment, which was her first sign that something was wrong.

Holly slipped out from behind him, her expression somber. Her best friend was incapable of hiding her emotions from her face.

Jace looked between them. "You guys are freaking me out with the faces. What's wrong?"

"There's someone you're gonna wanna talk to," Sam said. He nodded in the direction of the room he and Holly had just left.

"Okay," Jace said warily. Sam cleared a path for her, and she followed him out of the main room and into a small side room.

She noticed the waiter seated in a chair with his hands behind his back, and an officer hovering over him, and shot Sam a quizzical look. "Am I supposed to know him or something?"

"Jace," Holly began. "This is Gavin. He . . . he knows what happened to your brother."

Jace stared at her blankly for a second before the words sank in. "What do you mean he knows what happened? Like he saw it in the paper, or—"

"No. I mean he knows what happened because he was there."

Jace's chin started tremble as she fought back tears, and she looked at the stranger seated in the chair, the young man with swollen eyes and a hunched posture. "You know who hurt my brother?"

He refused to meet her eyes.

"Do you know who hurt my brother?" she asked again, emotion sharpening her voice.

He nodded.

Jace reached over and took Holly's hand, squeezing it for support. "I wanna know. Tell me what happened."

Gavin told her the events of that night, each detail sending fresh tears spilling down her cheeks. When he finished, he stared at the carpet while she cried.

"I'm sorry, he whispered.

"You're sorry?" Jace repeated, her voice thick with emotion. "My brother was found alone on the side of the road by someone on their way to work the next morning. If you were there that night, why didn't you help him? Why didn't you call an ambulance?"

When Gavin remained silent, she threw her purse at him, hitting him on the side of the head.

"Why didn't you help him!?" she screamed. She tried to find something else to throw at him, but Sam stepped in the way, and Holly wrapped her in a hug. "Why didn't you do something?" Jace sobbed, burying her face in her best friend's side. "Why?"

Ten

JACE COULD HEAR the speaker from the banquet hall as he began reading off the list of officers who had died the previous year, adding a few personal details to each name, but she didn't have the heart to care.

She stared at the note that had been slipped into her coat pocket, the letters bleeding together as her tears dropped onto the paper. "We always thought it was a hate crime."

Holly sat beside her, feet drawn up onto the chair, listening.

"But it wasn't. He was just on the wrong street. How does that even happen? What kind of monsters hurt people just for fun?"

Holly looked down at her red flats in silence. Sudden regret flooded Jace as she realized how callous that question must sound to someone who had lost her entire family at the hands of a sadistic serial killer.

"Oh, Holly, I'm sorry," she said. "I wasn't even thinking about your family."

Holly offered her a fragile smile. "You were thinking about your brother, which is who you should be thinking about."

At least I still have him, she thought with an unexpected flash of gratitude. She never thought she would be grateful that her baby brother was in a coma, but there was always a chance he might wake up and be a part of her life again.

Holly would never have that chance. All she would ever have were memories.

Jace crumpled the note in her fist. "It all seems so pointless. Your family, my brother. None of it had to happen. Your family died because some lunatic had mommy and daddy issues, and my brother's in a coma because four drunk teenagers were out looking for fun. And the one person who could've done something to help him, was too much of a coward, and he chose to stand by and do nothing. And then he left him there to die."

"I know it doesn't make what happened to Scott any better," Holly began, her voice quiet. "But to that girl who was being bullied, he made a world of difference."

"Yeah, I guess so. I wonder what her life is like, if she remembers what he did for her."

"She remembers." When Jace tossed a questioning glance her way, Holly explained, "We don't forget the people who stand up for us."

"You mean people like Mr. Southern?"

Holly's lips curled into a fleeting smile. "And Sam and Jordan." After a hesitation, she added quietly, "And Jacob." A moment of grief-filled silence stretched between them before Holly broke it. "Jacob's parents don't hate me. They're not even angry with me."

"Why would they be?" Jace asked.

"Because I'm the reason their son is dead."

Jace blinked in disbelief. "How can you think that?"

"How can I not?" Holly looked at her, her eyes shimmering. "When I refused to let Sam and Jacob inside, I was making a choice out of fear. I left them out there, Jace, knowing that there was a killer after me, knowing that he might try to go *through* Jacob or Sam to get to me, and that choice cost Jacob his life." Tears spilled down her cheeks. "My fear took Pat and Sally's only child from them. It took Marx's friend."

"Holly—"

"You said Gavin is a coward because he chose not to help your brother. He was so terrified of what would happen, that he couldn't see past his fear, and your brother paid the price for it. How am I any different?"

Holly's words slammed into Jace like an accusation, challenging what she had believed to be true just moments ago, and she floundered for an argument. "You're nothing like Gavin. You tried to help Jacob, remember?"

"After it was too late."

"That's not your fault. If you had tried to stop Edward from attacking Jacob, you might . . ." Jace's own words struck her, and she hesitated to finish them. "Be dead too."

If Gavin had intervened the night of her brother's attack, he might be the one in a coma—or worse. He had made a choice out of fear, just like Holly had when she forced Jacob to stand guard outside, and the consequences were devastating.

She would never have wanted Holly to endanger herself to save Jacob, but she expected a stranger to do just that for her brother. And not just a stranger, but a sixteen-year-old boy.

"Everyone says it's not my fault," Holly said, her voice distant, as if she were lost in a memory. "But I feel it."

Jace had seen the same pain and regret on Gavin's face that she saw on her best friend's now—a longing to go back and make a different choice—and it unsettled her.

She was so angry with Gavin, and she wanted someone to blame. But deep down, she recognized the truth God was whispering through Holly's words: Gavin was no more responsible for her brother's attack than Holly was for Jacob's death.

He had only been a child when faced with that terrifying situation, and he was already living with regrets.

Jace threw an irritated glance toward Heaven. *Sometimes You can be really pushy, You know that? You couldn't just let me have my anger for a little while? Let me hate him?*

Of course not. Because God understood things that she couldn't in the midst of her anger, like the fact that her best friend was hurting, and that her bitter comments about Gavin had only deepened Holly's sense of guilt.

Jace let out a breath as she searched for the words to undo the damage she'd caused. "I was wrong, Holly." Those words tasted sour on her tongue, but she pressed on. "I'm angry about what happened to Scott, and no one has ever been held accountable for what was done to him. Hearing the details of that night . . . I wanted someone to blame."

Truth be told, she was still a little angry, and she was going to be doing some digging into a guy named Vic.

"But—"

"What happened to Jacob is not your fault. His parents are right. I know you feel responsible because you have this whole weight of the world on your shoulders thing going on, which by the way, is really unhealthy, and you have very small shoulders, so . . ." she cut herself off before she could wander off on a tangent. "Jacob volunteered to protect you, and I'm sure he knew it would put his life in danger. Regardless of what *your* choice was, that was *his* choice."

She wrapped her fingers around Holly's and squeezed.

"Maybe tomorrow you could go with me to talk to Gavin again. I think I should hear the story again, and maybe listen to his side this time," Jace said.

"Sure."

Jace blew out a breath and shrugged the tension from her shoulders. "Good. I'm glad that conversation's over." She brushed her fingers under her eyes and frowned at the black substance coating her fingertips. "Great, my mascara's running."

"Mine's not."

Jace rolled her eyes. "That's because you're not wearing any. No makeup, no stilettos. And seriously, what's with the sweater?"

Holly looked down at her sweater in confusion. "What's wrong with it?"

"It's huge. I feel like if I push you, you'll ring like a Christmas bell."

Holly snorted a laugh as she dried her tears. "It's not that bad."

"Oh, it's that bad. You definitely look like you're trying to hide a prego belly. Mr. Too-much-wine had at least one thing right." She cocked her head in thought. "Do you think Marx threw him headfirst into a snow drift when he dragged him outside? Because that would be awesome."

Holly grinned. "I wouldn't put it past him."

"Holly." Both girls twisted in their seats to look at the source of the southern voice. Marx stood in the doorway to the room with Sam behind him, and his expression was . . . unhappy.

"I didn't do it," Holly said quickly.

Marx folded his arms. "What exactly didn't you do?"

"Mm, whatever it was that put that look on your face?"

Marx's eyebrows lifted. "I see. So it was just some girl who looked *exactly* like you who ran out the door into the night, puttin' herself in danger."

Holly bit her bottom lip and glanced at Jace. "I'm hungry. Are you hungry?"

"Totally. I heard there's a dessert table to die for."

Holly perked up at the mention of dessert, and Marx fought not to let his reprimanding grimace slip into a smile. She hopped out of her chair but paused a few feet from the doorway when he didn't immediately move. She looked up at him, her brown eyes a picture of innocence, and his irritation evaporated.

He stepped aside with a sigh. "Go." She was already slipping through the crowd toward the table of sweets, when he hollered, "And no more runnin' outside!"

Eleven

WHEN MARX ARRIVED AT the dining table with his plate of food, he found Holly sitting with her back to the exit—probably for a quick escape, if necessary—and the chair two spaces to her right pulled out.

"I saved you a seat," she said with a grin.

"Didn't I tell you not to pull out my chair?"

"Maybe."

"Mmm hmm." He pushed the chair back under the edge of the table, walked past it, and sat down in the vacant chair next to her. He set his plate of food on the table and picked up his sandwich.

When Holly scowled at him like a dissatisfied toddler, and scooted her chair a few feet away from him, he had to hold back a laugh to keep from choking on his food. She had the most dramatic scowl. He half-expected her to stand up, place her hands on her hips, and stomp her foot in outrage. Thankfully, she didn't, or he *would've* choked.

She took a bite of a cookie, and Marx noticed her plate of food for the first time. She had a slice of cherry pie surrounded by a wall of cookies, with a brownie plopped on top.

"Really?" he asked.

She looked at her plate of sweets and then back up at him. "What?"

"Did you miss the table of real food?"

"This *is* real food. I have something from every food group, see?" She pointed to the items on her plate. "Chocolate, whipped cream, pie—"

"No, those are cavities, not food groups."

She eyed his plate of vegetables, fruits, and a sandwich. "You're just jealous because your food's boring." She took another nibble of her cookie, then asked, "So, you remember when you offered to teach me how to drive?"

"Mmm hmm."

She hesitated, as if afraid she might not get the answer she was hoping for. "Did . . . you mean it?"

Her doubt that he would keep his word bothered him, and made him wonder if he was the first person in her life to follow through with his promises. "Of course I mean it."

Her eyes filled with a cautious hope that caused a flicker of pain in his chest. She was twenty-eight-years old, and the world had been so cruel that it left her wary of kindness and honesty, expecting violence and lies to follow. It made him want to find the people who hurt her and make them regret it.

"When can we start? Can we start tonight?" she asked.

He smiled at her eagerness. "Not legally, no. And seein' as I'm a cop, we should probably do things the legal way."

"Oh. How long does that take?"

"We'll get you a permit, and maybe we can start tomorrow."

She brightened. "Really?"

"Really. Just as soon as you eat somethin' other than sugar." He shifted some of his fruit and vegetables over to a napkin and slid it toward her. "Try somethin' nutritious for once."

She wrinkled her nose. "But I don't like vegetables."

"I've noticed." Considering he had never seen her eat one. "But I don't like sugar junkies drivin' my car."

She narrowed her eyes at him. "There's no such thing as a sugar junkie." When he looked pointedly at her plate, she did too. Maybe he had a point. "So . . . if I eat . . . these,"—she picked up a baby carrot and studied it—"you'll teach me to drive tomorrow?"

"That's the idea."

She stared at the carrot, considering whether or not driving lessons were worth the death of her taste buds. "This feels like manipulation."

"I prefer to call it a bargain." He popped a few grapes into his mouth as he watched her.

She heaved a sigh and crunched off a bite of carrot. Her face scrunched in disgust, and she chewed methodically before swallowing. Marx laughed as she chased every bite of carrot down with two bites of a chocolate chip cookie.

It looked like they were going to start driving lessons tomorrow. Hopefully, his car would survive.

C.C. Warrens

The End

A Brief Glimpse into Cross Fire . . .

CROSS FIRE

1

The aroma of sweat and coconut shampoo filled the room, bringing to mind a tropical sweat lodge. I paced the outside of the rubber mat, casting wary looks at my opponent.

He was roughly ten inches taller than me—putting him at an even six feet—and he had a lean muscular build that made my runner's physique pale by comparison. His eyes, which reminded me of a clear blue sky, sparkled with amusement as he watched me.

"You actually have to get close to me to hit me, Holly," he pointed out.

My hands were sheathed in fingerless purple boxing gloves, and I interlaced my fingers, twisting them anxiously in front of my stomach. I reached the end of the mat and spun on my heel to pace back in the other direction.

Up until this point, our training had been entirely nonphysical. I had mirrored his movements, albeit less gracefully, from a safe distance. We had touched on the possibility of sparring during our last lesson, but I wasn't ready to plunge into it.

"I'm not sure—"

"Jordan's not gonna hurt you, Holly," a smooth voice with a touch of Southern said from the back of the room.

I glanced at Marx, who leaned against the wall by the door, arms folded and ankles crossed in a relaxed position. He was wearing jeans and a black T-shirt—his casual wear for when he wasn't on duty—but as an NYPD detective, he was never truly *off* duty. He always carried his gun and badge in case he was called away unexpectedly to a crime scene.

I doubted I would ever truly feel safe with a man, but I trusted Marx more than any other man. He knew my secrets and my fears, and he was always mindful of them. He understood that I wasn't comfortable being alone with Jordan yet, and he made it a point always to be here with me.

"I'm not gonna grab you," Jordan assured me. "We're not there yet. We'll work on breaking out of holds when you're more comfortable with it."

When I was more comfortable with it . . . right. So, never? Yep, I was comfortable with never.

"I'm gonna stand perfectly still." He held out his hands shoulder-width apart in front of him.

I sighed and walked across the mat in my workout toe socks. I stopped four feet from him. We had an agreement: he remained at least four feet from me at all times except in an emergency, and we didn't touch one another. He was asking me to break that agreement . . . and then punch him.

"Can we just go back to mirroring the movements? I like that better," I said.

"I can teach you the punches, kicks, and blocks until you can do them in your sleep, but it doesn't teach you how to connect them or how to recover if you miss. It also doesn't teach you how to dodge if someone is trying to hit you."

The last time someone had taken a swing at me, I had curled into a ball on the floor and covered my head with my arms. That sort of counted as dodging, right?

"This is important, Holly," Marx said. I met his eyes and saw worry swirling in their green depths.

He knew as well as I did that Collin hadn't decided to pack up and leave; he would view the cops surrounding me as a challenge, and he savored a challenge.

Collin was my foster brother, the only biological child of the foster family who took me in when I was fourteen, and he had developed an unhealthy fascination with me.

I had spent the past ten years in hiding—moving from city to city, working odd jobs under the table, never drawing attention to myself—in the hopes that he wouldn't find me.

I had managed to hide from him for two years in New York City, but then I made a mistake: I gave a statement to the police after two men attacked me in the park, all but lighting up a blinking neon sign that read, "Holly is here."

The statement I gave to the cops, which was logged into a "secure" police database, was accessed by an outside source. I didn't doubt for a moment my foster brother was behind the breach of their system.

He hadn't made an appearance yet, but he had called me on my birthday a month ago just to let me know he was watching.

I knew what he would do to me if he got his hands on me again, and I couldn't let that happen. I had decided not to run this time, which meant my only hope was learning how to fight.

I tapped my fingers on my hips nervously as I looked at Jordan. "What if I hurt you?"

His lips twitched in amusement. "You're not gonna hurt me. You're not gonna hurt anyone from that far away." He motioned me closer with his fingers. "Come on. Across the border."

When we first met—or rather, re-met—in Kansas this past November, he had jokingly dubbed the invisible personal bubble around me "the border."

I chewed on my lower lip and then crossed over the invisible boundary. I pushed my red braid back over my shoulder and sank into the stance we'd practiced for the past three weeks.

"Make sure you don't bend your wrist too much. And focus on the form of your punch rather than the strength of it for the first few swings. Here's your target." He waved his right hand.

I folded my fingers into a fist and planted it gently into his gloved palm. I repeated the movement a few more times, practicing until I felt confident I wouldn't accidentally miss and punch him in the face.

"Okay, let's see what you've got," he said.

I exhaled heavily and then swatted his open palm with my fist. When he didn't say anything, I hit his hand again.

"I think I just got high-fived by a gnat," he commented, completely deadpan. "Put a little force behind it, Holly. Hit me like you mean it."

I glared at him, and he gave me one of his trademark charming yet playful smiles. I smacked my fist into his hand again, and he arched a blond eyebrow at me, which apparently meant "punch harder."

"I think he's doubtin' your abilities, Holly," Marx said, and I glanced over at him. He inclined his head in a silent signal.

I darted forward, kicked Jordan in the back of his knee, and swept his legs out from under him while he was off balance. I scampered out of reach as his back slapped the mat.

He wheezed in surprise and then unexpectedly started to laugh. "Seriously?" He propped himself up on his elbows and looked at me. I grinned, and his gaze slid to Marx. "I did not teach her that."

Marx smiled proudly. "I taught her that."

He and Sam, his friend and fellow officer, had demonstrated that technique for me repeatedly until I was able to simulate it solo. Jordan was the first person I had tried it on. I hadn't expected it to go so well.

Honestly, I thought I would trip myself.

Jordan sighed as he sat up on the mat. "I just got taken out by a 110-pound woman. That stings a bit."

"As it should," Marx informed him.

"Yeah, well, I'm ready this time." Jordan climbed to his feet and made a show of brushing off his clothes before looking at me. "No more cheap shots."

I hesitated at the edge of the mat, anxiety sparking in my stomach. "You're not gonna retaliate, are you?" The last thing I wanted was to be body-slammed on the mat for taking his legs out from under him.

"Not if he wants to keep breathin'," Marx muttered under his breath.

Mischief danced in Jordan's eyes. "I'm not gonna retaliate. But I do think you owe me an ice cream cone for bruising my ego."

My eyebrows crept up. "It's twenty-three degrees out."

"Then I guess we won't have to worry about it melting." He held up his hands again. "Left hook this time."

Satisfied that he wasn't going to tackle me or twist me into some sort of pretzel in retaliation, I walked across the mat to join him.

"Try putting your body behind it this time," he suggested. "You're not getting enough force by just using your arms."

I shifted my stance a little, trying to figure out what he meant by putting my body behind it. I was pretty sure that if I was punching someone, my body was naturally behind my arm.

"Do what I do, okay?" He raised his fists and demonstrated a right hook. He moved as fluidly as water, and I pitied anyone who came in contact with the other end of that punch.

I tried to mirror him, but after watching his easy movements, I felt as inflexible as a stick. I wondered if I could even touch my toes without bending my knees. I glanced down at them, curious, and decided I would have to try that later.

"Twist with the punch," he said.

"I *am* twisting!"

"No, you're turning your whole body."

"What's the difference?" I demanded irritably.

I watched him a few more times, trying each time to make my body do what his did. Judging by the frown line between his blond eyebrows, I was failing.

"Don't step forward. Keep your back foot behind you, and just move from the core up," he explained.

I could throw a decent punch if I stood perfectly still. How was I supposed to concentrate on swinging without bending my wrist too much, not moving my feet, and twisting but not turning all at the same time?

"Why can't I just use my fists?" I huffed in frustration.

He bit back a sigh and ran a hand through his hair. "Because you'll be lucky to knock out a mosquito, let alone an actual person."

I glared at him.

"Here, just let me . . ." He reached forward and his fingers grazed my waist before I danced back beyond his reach with a flutter of fear.

"You said no grabbing!"

He froze where he stood, and realization flickered across his features. "I'm sorry." He stepped back with his hands raised. "I didn't mean to invade your space. I just forgot."

I wrapped my arms protectively around my midsection and tried to ignore the anxiety crawling the walls of my stomach.

Jordan tried to respect my boundaries, but he had a difficult time remembering I wasn't as free with touch as most people. What might be a casual or unconscious gesture for others could twist my nerves into knots.

Marx peeled away from the wall and said, "Okay, we're done for the day."

Jordan opened his mouth like he wanted to object, but then exhaled and dropped his arms in defeat. "Yeah, okay."

His expression was a meld of confusion and regret. He didn't understand my fear, and I didn't think I could explain it to him.

"We'll work on it more next time," he said. He offered me a smile that was too thin to be reassuring and then left the room.

I dropped back against the wall and slid to the floor, frustration and disappointment clinging to me.

Marx sat down beside me and leaned back against the wall with his legs stretched out in front of him. He always gave me space without me having to ask.

"You did good today," he said.

"I don't think we're remembering the same lesson, because that"—I gestured to the room—"was a disaster."

He gave me a gentle smile. "No, it just feels that way because you're frustrated with yourself." He was quiet for a moment before saying, "It's okay to be scared, Holly. It's okay to need space. After everythin' you've been through, nobody expects you to just *get over it*."

I averted my eyes and rubbed at the palms of my gloves.

"You've made a lot of progress. It's been what, four and a half months since you've considered slammin' a door in my face?"

I smiled at the memory.

We had met in October when a serial killer was stalking me. I had vehemently disliked him due to the fact that he was a man, a cop, and imposing at five feet ten with a gun. When he'd shown up at my apartment the next day with more questions, I had very much wanted to slam my door in his face.

Now I considered him a friend.

"You never thought you could trust a cop, let alone a man. Now here I am sittin' about two feet from you and you're not even scared," he observed.

I looked at the doorway Jordan had disappeared through. "It's . . . harder with him than it is with you."

I was trying to rekindle the friendship Jordan and I had as children, but there was an insurmountable barrier between us. And it wasn't the eighteen years we had spent apart.

"It's because you know he's attracted to you," Marx said after a thoughtful pause. At my surprised look, he gave me a sad, knowing smile. "You curl in on yourself whenever you think about intimacy, like you're subconsciously tryin' to protect yourself."

I hadn't realized I had wrapped my arms around my stomach and drawn my knees into my chest until he pointed it out. I tried to force my body to relax.

Marx was in no way attracted to me— maybe because he was forty-seven and I was twenty-eight—and it made me feel safer with him. But Jordan had made it clear that he was, and I was on guard every moment we were in the same room together.

"It'll work itself out. You just have to be patient with yourself," Marx said. "Now come on. Let's go get a terribly unhealthy lunch before I drop you off at home. It'll make you feel better."

"Tacos?"

"If that's what you want."

"And sombrero-sized tortilla chips with cheese dip?" I asked hopefully.

He laughed. "Of course." He stood and offered me his hand, but I ignored it as usual. One of these days I would let him help me up, just to see the look of surprise on his face.

Check out Cross Fire for the continuation.

About the Author

Jesus and laughter have brought C.C. through some very difficult times in life, and she weaves both into every story she writes, creating a world of breath-stealing intensity, laugh-out-loud humor, and a sparkle of hope.

Writing has been a slowly blossoming dream inside her for most of her life until one day it spilled out onto the pages that would become her first published book. If she's not writing, she's attempting to bake something—however catastrophic that might be—or she's enjoying the beauty of the outdoors with her husband.

One of the many things she's learned since she started this journey is that the best way to write a book is to go on a long stroll with her husband. That is when the characters—from their backgrounds to the moments that make them laugh or bubble over with anger—come to life.

How to Connect

Facebook: https://www.facebook.com/ccwarrens
Website: https://www.ccwarrensbooks.com/
Email: ccwarrens@yahoo.com

Winter Memorial

Every dream starts as a flicker of hope for something more. Let that tiny hope shine, and someday it may light up the world.

Winter Memorial

Made in the USA
Columbia, SC
30 April 2020